For Lucy, Terry, and John

Mary Wormell

WHY NOT?

A SUNBURST BOOK · FARRAR STRAUS GIROUX

"**C**ome on, time for supper," called Barnaby's mom,

as she set off toward the house.

"Don't chase the chickens, Barnaby!" she called.

"WHY NOT?" Barnaby asked.

"Because I'll chase YOU," crowed the rooster.

"But I can climb out of your way," cried Barnaby,
as he started up the tree.

"Don't scare the birds, Barnaby!" called his mom.
"WHY NOT?"

"Because I'll scare YOU," cawed the crow.

"But I can leap out of your way," cried Barnaby,
as he sprang down from the tree.

"Don't annoy the sheep, Barnaby!" called his mom.
"WHY NOT?"

"Because I'll annoy YOU!" snorted the ram.

"But I can jump out of your way," cried Barnaby,
as he bounded over the fence.

"Don't frighten the foal, Barnaby!" called his mom.
"WHY NOT?"

"Because I'll frighten YOU!" neighed the horse.

"But I can get out of your way," cried Barnaby,
as he squeezed under the hay bales.

"Don't squeeze in there, Barnaby!" called his mom.
"WHY NOT?"

"Because you will get stuck!" warned his mom.

"BUT I AM STUCK!" cried Barnaby.

"We will help you," offered the rooster, the crow, the ram, and the horse eagerly.

"Don't!" meowed Barnaby, as he struggled to get free.
"WHY NOT?" they called, as they moved toward him.

"Because . . ." cried Barnaby, as he struggled even harder.

"Because . . . I'm already . . .

. . . OUT!"

And he ran up the garden path and back to
his mom in time for supper.

Library of Congress Cataloging-in-Publication Data

Wormell, Mary.

Why not? / Mary Wormell.

    p.   cm.

    Summary: When his mother repeatedly tells him not to bother the other animals, Barnaby
the kitten always asks: "Why not?"

    ISBN 0-374-48384-1 (pbk.)

    [1. Cats—Fiction.   2. Domestic animals—Fiction.   3. Animals—Infancy—Fiction.]   I. Title.

PZ7.W88774Wh 2000

[E]—dc21

99-27163